The Little Mouse That Could
A Tale of Believing in Yourself

Mason Melotakis

Once upon a time in a cozy
little farmhouse,
Lived a tiny little creature
the size of a mouse.

He scurried around, both day
and night,
Always seeking adventure, oh
what a sight!

One day he came across a potion so rare,
In a bottle with a liquid so shiny does he dare?

He decided to take a sip and
to his surprise,
He suddenly felt big and
mighty oh, how he could rise!

Before he felt tiny in a forest
so grand,
with towering trees, like a
magical land.

But though he was small, he
felt quite large,
Thanks to the potion he was
in charge.

He danced and he twirled, oh
what a show,
with animals watching, all in
a row.

They gasped in awe at his
magical trick,
The potion's powers making
him quick.

With envy he saw the birds
high above,
wishing he too could fly like a
dove.

So he decided to get some
wings of his own,
A little mouse that could
fly...who would have known?

Through a maze filled with cheese he finished the race with the potion's powers, he set the pace.

No obstacle too big, no challenge too tough, The little mouse was more than enough!

With a heart so kind, he helped
a bunny in need,
Guiding it home was a selfless
deed.

The potion may be magic, that
is true,
But kindness and courage, he
had them too.

Back in his house, all cozy and snug,
He laid in bed, with a yawn and a shrug.

Dreaming of adventures that
lay ahead,
He was now optimistic, he had
no dread.

Little did he know the potion
had no powers at all
In fact it was simply water,
but today small didnt seem
so small

He had the courage within him
all along,
Next time you think you
can't...remember you're
strong!

Always Believe in Yourself!

The End

Made in the USA
Coppell, TX
11 April 2024

31159254R00024